FRIGHTFUL FAMILIES

For Billy Pinnock,
the best left foot in Brighton.
S.M.
For Chris.
T.M.

ORCHARD BOOKS
338 Euston Road, London NW1 3BH
Orchard Books Australia
Hachette Children's Books
Level 17/207 Kent St, Sydney, NSW 2000
ISBN 1 84362 568 7 (hardback)
ISBN 1 84362 576 8 (paperback)
First published in Great Britain in 2006
First paperback publication in 2007
Text © Sue Mongredien 2006
Illustrations © Teresa Murfin 2006
The rights of Sue Mongredien to be identified as the author
and of Teresa Murfin to be identified as the illustrator of this work
have been asserted by them in accordance with the
Copyright, Designs and Patents Act, 1988.
A CIP catalogue record for this book is available
from the British Library.
1 3 5 7 9 10 8 6 4 2 (hardback)
1 3 5 7 9 10 8 6 4 2 (paperback)
Printed in Great Britain by Mackays of Chatham plc, Chatham, Kent.
www.wattspublishing.co.uk

FRIGHTFUL FAMILIES

FOOTBALL-MAD DAD

SUE MONGREDIEN • TERESA MURFIN

ORCHARD BOOKS

Jake Jones was a fabulous footballer. His scoring was superb. His free kicks were fantastic. His passing was so perfect, it brought tears to his teacher's eyes. But it wasn't really surprising when you saw his dad.

Mr Jones LOVED football. His favourite
team were the local side, Donchester Rovers.
Every Saturday afternoon, he'd go to watch
them, home or away, cheering, shouting,
sometimes even crying.

Jake knew other dads who were football fans. But Mr Jones was a fanatic! He had painted their front room in the Rovers' red and white stripes. The kitchen and bathroom were decorated with red and white tiles.

As for the Jones's car...well, there was no mistaking *that*.

Once, Mr Jones had even dyed his hair red and white. He had his picture in the paper and everything. But when it rained, his hair turned...a lovely shade of pink! After that, he decided to leave it brown.

... well as supporting Donchester Rovers, Mr Jones had a second favourite team: Donchester Primary.

Donchester Primary was Jake's school team. Week in, week out, Mr Jones was there without fail...unfortunately for Jake.

It wasn't that Jake didn't *want* his dad to come along. In some ways, it was great to have a football-mad dad. Who else would be willing to practise penalties with him for hours on end in the park?

Who else would save up for weeks to get his son the best football boots that money could buy?

Most of the time, Jake was glad his dad was a football fanatic. He just wished he didn't have to be quite so...*loud* about it.

"Go on, son, get stuck in!" Mr Jones would shout from the touchline.

Jake would see his dad leaping about, red-faced, all on his own except for the PE teacher's dog. Then he couldn't help wishing his dad had another hobby. Something far, far away from the school football pitch.

Jake's mum, on the other hand, wasn't interested in football at all. Music was her thing. She loved singing and playing instruments. She had trained as an opera singer when she was younger and still sang in some local shows. She also ran a kids' music club at Jake's school.

Mr Jones was rather scornful about music. "Anybody can shake a tambourine," he would say. "And anyone can whistle a tune. But it takes real skill to curl a free kick, eh, Jakey boy?"

Jake tried not to answer that one. For he and his mum shared a secret. As well as being a fabulous footballer, Jake was also a musical marvel.

Every Monday evening, Mr Jones went to the pub to watch the big match on telly with all his mates.

And every Monday evening, Jake went along with his mum to her after-school music club.

At first, he had just sat on the side, reading a book or playing a computer game. But after a few weeks, he had started listening.

He listened as little Helena Hayes hit the high notes in her solo.

He listened as gentle Jenny Jackson bashed out a beat on the bongo drums until her hands were a blur.

And he listened as Lily Lane shook her shakers with such rhythm that her whole body bopped to the music.

And as he listened, he realised that he rather liked it.

Then, one day, Jake's mum was teaching her class a complicated song. Nobody could quite get the hang of it.

"No, Jenny," Mrs Jones said patiently. "The beat goes: dum-dum-dum-DAH-dum, dum-DAH-dum. Got it?"

Jenny frowned, then started drumming. *Dum DAH-dum, dum-dum dum* her hands went.

"Nearly," Mrs Jones said. She went over to tap it out next to her. *Dum-dum-dum-DAH dum, dum-DAH-dum. Dum-dum-dum-DAH dum, dum-DAH-dum...*

"Can you hear the difference?" she asked Jenny.

Jenny still looked confused. "Um..." she said. "I think so."

At the back of the hall, Jake's footballer feet were twitching. *Dum-dum-dum-DAH-dum*, his toes tapped. *Dum-DAH-dum*.

He found that his fingers were patting out the rhythm on his knees, louder and louder. He forgot that anyone else was there, and concentrated on the sound he was making. *Dum-dum-dum-DAH-dum, dum-DAH-dum...*

Then he looked around to see the whole of the class staring at him. "Well I never!" his mum said proudly. "Why don't you take this set of drums and join in?" Her eyes were twinkling. "I think you might be a natural."

That was how it started. And now, months later, Jake couldn't only play the drums with terrific timing, he could strum a few tunes on the guitar.

He was learning the violin, too.

As for his singing...well. His singing was something else.

When Jake and Helena sang together, the whole room fell silent. Mrs Jones got goosebumps just listening to them.

Jake loved music. Soon, Monday evenings became the best part of the week. Better than football. Better even than Friday night fish and chips!

Although he adored his music lessons, Jake begged his mum to keep it a secret. He knew that his football-mad dad would only laugh.

"*Music?*" Jake could imagine him snorting. "Don't waste your time, son. Footballers don't muck about with violins! Not when there are goals to be scored!"

The only music Jake's dad liked was the singing on the football terraces.

So Jake said nothing. It was easier that way.

One Saturday, Jake's team were playing the Donchester Prep School. Jake's school and the Donny Prep lads were bitter rivals. Both teams had good players and Jake knew it was going to be a tough match. "PEEP!" went the whistle, and the game began.

Jake passed back to Liam, the centre-half. Liam kicked the ball out to the wing. Jake ran like a racehorse to get in a good position for goal. Ryan, their winger, crossed the ball to the centre. Jake kept his eye on the ball and...

"SHOOT, son! Put it away!"

There was his dad behind the goal-mouth, bellowing orders as usual. Jake took his eye off the ball for a second, and...

WHAM! One of the Donny Prep defenders had booted the ball back down the pitch.

"That was a *sitter*!" his dad howled in horror. "How did you miss that?"

"Sorry," Jake muttered to his team-mates. What was wrong with him? Normally he'd have slammed a ball like that straight in the back of the net. He tried not to groan as his dad started barking instructions from the sideline.

"Eye on the ball, son. Got to keep your EYE on the ball!"

Some of the Donny Prep boys were staring at Mr Jones. "Who does he think he is – the England manager?" someone sniggered.

Jake tried to ignore them, but he was rattled. The next time Ryan tried to pass the ball to him, Jake fluffed it again, letting it roll straight to a Donny Prep defender.

He was all over the place. He was playing like a puppy dog. His feet just weren't doing what he wanted them to do!

"What's wrong with you, boy?" came the shout from the side. "Focus, Jake. FOCUS!" Jake gritted his teeth.

"Don't forget to focus, will you?" teased a Donny Prep boy. "Focus, Jake, focus!"

"I'll focus you in a minute," Jake growled, running off to help defend. The truth was, he was finding it impossible to focus on anything. Not with his motor-mouth dad running up and down the sidelines. He seemed louder than ever today. Even professional players would struggle to focus with a dad like that!

Then something awful happened. One of the Donny Prep strikers was brought down in the box. Penalty!

Before the ball was even placed on the spot, Mr Jones was on the pitch.

"You've got to be joking, ref," he yelled in outrage, striding across to the referee. "Don't you know a dive when you see one? Cheats, that's what those prep school boys are – cheats!"

There was a terrible silence. Then the referee fumbled in his pocket and pulled out a red card. "Get off this pitch at once!" he ordered Mr Jones. He brandished the red card in his face. "Off! You are banned from watching the rest of this match. You've been causing a disturbance ever since it started."

Mr Jones' mouth fell open. Then he said, "You can't give me the red card. I'm not even playing!"

"Exactly," the referee fumed. "So do us all a favour and leave the pitch. NOW!"

Both teams watched as Mr Jones made his way back to the sidelines.

"You can watch the rest of the match from the school," the referee said. "I don't want to hear another peep out of you!"

Mr Jones opened his mouth to protest, but instead he straightened his red and white bobble hat, and walked all the way over to the school building. Then he pulled out a pair of binoculars, and did a thumbs up at everybody.

Jake thought he was about to fall over with embarrassment.

"Whose dad is THAT?" someone from the other team sniggered.

Even his team-mates were making comments. "About time the ref got rid of him," they said. "He does my head in, shouting at us every week."

Jake played out the rest of the match as if he was sleep-walking through a terrible dream. They lost, 3-0. It was the worst game of his life. As soon as the final whistle blew, Jake's dad rushed over.

"I couldn't help noticing your corners weren't up to scratch today, Jake," he said.

"You passed like a pussy cat. You tackled like a tortoise. And as for your marking – that defender was all over you!"

Jake's shoulders slumped. Everything his dad said was true. He hadn't played well at all. But even the best players had off days. Why couldn't his dad give him a break?

"Jake's been too busy with his violin, I reckon," Liam said, pulling on some tracksuit pants.

Jake's ears turned red and he held his breath, hoping his dad hadn't heard. "Come on, Dad, let's go," he said quickly.

"Violin?" Mr Jones echoed, staring at Liam with a puzzled expression.

Jake pulled him away. "Come on," he repeated.

"Did he just say 'violin'?" his dad asked.

"Didn't you know?" Liam said. "Our Jakey's the star violinist at school. Aren't you, Jake?"

The walk home was very silent. Mr Jones looked thunder-struck.

"I was going to tell you," Jake muttered. "The headteacher has asked me to play the violin in the school concert."

"But you're a footballer!" his dad spluttered. His red and white scarf trailed miserably behind him. "Footballers don't play the violin! Haven't I taught you anything?"

Jake sighed. He didn't know what to say.

His dad shook his head. "What am I going to tell the lads? You're – a violinist? I've told them all you're going to play for the Rovers! And now...this! Talk about embarrassing."

"Embarrassing? *Me?*" Jake couldn't keep the shock out of his voice. "You think *I'm* the embarrassing one?"

They were almost at their house by now.
"Dad – *you* embarrass *me*. All the time!"
Jake blurted out. "Our stupid red and white
car. Your stupid red and white hair. As for all
those school football matches you come to…"

"I'm supporting you!" Mr Jones protested. "I'm giving you advice, I'm..."

"You're embarrassing me," Jake said bluntly. Then he walked up to their front door and let himself in.

Mr Jones stood in the street for a few moments. He looked as shocked as he had when Melbury Town had beaten Donchester Rovers 6-0. Him – an embarrassment? How could that possibly be true?

He was quiet all the way through lunch.

He was quiet all the way through the Rovers' match that afternoon.

He was even quiet when they beat Wilton Wanderers 2-1. For the first time in years, he was thinking about something other than football. He was thinking about Jake.

Next Saturday, as Jake wandered down the stairs, the house felt very quiet.

"I'll drop you off at the match today," his mum said. "Your dad's gone to the garden centre. Says he's going to get a new hobby."

"Dad's...not coming?" Jake gasped. He could hardly believe it. But it was true.

The school match was strange without
Mr Jones there. Strange...and very peaceful.
It was almost relaxing, without all the
usual shouting.

Jake played well with no one distracting him. He scored a cracking goal in the first half, then another two in the second half. Hat-trick!

"That's nice, dear," his mum said on
the way home when he told her. "Shall we
have sausages for lunch?"

It was the start of an amazing change. Over the next few weeks, Mr Jones became a different man. Calmer. Quieter. A whole lot more normal. He still practised football with Jake, and asked him questions about the school matches.

But on Saturday mornings, he tended his garden instead of watching Jake play. After a few weeks, his red and white roses were looking lovely.

Then came the evening of the school concert. Jake hadn't mentioned it again to his dad. He thought it might upset him. He knew his dad had been disappointed to hear that his own son wasn't as football-mad as him – so why rub his nose in it?

"Boys and girls, mums and dads, I'm proud to present our violin virtuoso – Jake Jones!" the headteacher announced.

Everybody clapped as Jake walked nervously on stage. He tucked the violin under his chin, stretched out his bow and...

"Go on, my son! Give it some WELLY!
We are the champions!"

There was his dad, standing up in the
middle of the front row, waving a brand-new
scarf in the air.

Jake watched as his mum dragged his dad down again. Then Jake smiled.

Maybe his dad was always going to behave like a football fanatic, whether he was at a match or not. But he was here today. He had come to see Jake, his son, play the violin. Who would have thought it?

Jake found that he was beaming at his dad. Mr Jones winked back and gave him a double thumbs up. Then Jake played the most beautiful music he'd ever played in his life. And *everybody* cheered.

FRIGHTFUL FAMILIES

WRITTEN BY SUE MONGREDIEN • ILLUSTRATED BY TERESA MURFIN

Explorer Trauma	1 84362 571 7
Headmaster Disaster	1 84362 572 5
Millionaire Mayhem	1 84362 573 3
Clown Calamity	1 84362 574 1
Popstar Panic	1 84362 575 X
Football-mad Dad	1 84362 576 8
Chef Shocker	1 84362 577 6
Astronerds	1 84362 803 1

All priced at £3.99

Frightful Families are available from all good bookshops, or can be ordered direct from the publisher: Orchard Books, PO BOX 29, Douglas IM99 1BQ
Credit card orders please telephone 01624 836000
or fax 01624 837033 or visit our Internet site: www.wattspub.co.uk
or e-mail: bookshop@enterprise.net for details.

To order please quote title, author and ISBN
and your full name and address.
Cheques and postal orders should be made payable to 'Bookpost plc.'
Postage and packing is FREE within the UK
(overseas customers should add £1.00 per book).
Prices and availability are subject to change.